THE *B*ENEFICIARY

TRANSLATED BY ROSLYN THEOBALD

in Collaboration with the Author

THE *B*ENEFICIARY

BARBARA *K*ÖNIG

NORTHWESTERN UNIVERSITY PRESS

Evanston, Illinois

Northwestern
University Press
Evanston, Illinois
60208-4210

First published
in German as *Der
Beschenkte*.
Copyright © 1980
by Carl Hanser Verlag.
English translation
copyright © 1993 by
Northwestern University
Press. All rights reserved

Printed in the United
States of America

The paper used in
this publication meets
the minimum require-
ments of the American
National Standard for
Information Sciences—
Permanence of Paper
for Printed Library
Materials,
ANSI Z39.48-1984

Library of Congress
Cataloging-in-Publication Data
König, Barbara, 1925–
    [Beschenkte. English]
    The beneficiary / Barbara König ;
[translated by Roslyn Theobald in collaboration with the author].
    p.   cm.
    ISBN 0-8101-1105-5
    I. Title.
PT2671.023B413   1993
833'.914—dc20   93-11960
                                        CIP

THE BENEFICIARY

We Are Gathered Here to Honor a Man

Thirty-five years ago today Chaplain Johann Schorr sacrificed his life for the life of a man sentenced to death before a military tribunal.

We are gathered here to honor a man.

The sentenced man, a young soldier, survived the war. We welcome him to this celebration.

Mommsen on the podium in the heat of the spotlights, serious, respectful, appearing as he is expected to appear. He is not the hero, he is merely the man who made another man a hero, the negative half so to speak. Holding his hat in his hand he stands with bowed head next to the lectern while the mayor delivers his remarks, and from behind Mommsen, from behind a black frame, the slightly protruding eyes of the priest look down on him kindly. Mommsen just stands there, devoid of any thought.

We want to thank you for coming.

Mommsen is led into the pressroom. They surround him without getting too close; it is as if he had a contagious disease or the odor of a victim who is beyond rescue.

They keep their distance even when they are seated at the table. They cross their legs and lean back in their chairs. Mommsen is the only one sitting up straight, his elbows resting on the arms of his chair. This way he is less exposed.

He has no reason to be afraid. He is nothing more than the evidence of another man's saintliness, and the mere fact of his existence will suffice as evidence. It will suffice that he is neither a criminal nor a simpleton, nor in any other way a blemish on mankind.

How Did You Do It?

What does this celebration mean to you?

This deed, this sacrifice?

This man, Father Johann Schorr?

And you weren't especially close?

You weren't his confidante, his friend?

But you did know the three others in your cell, the ones who had to die because no one was there to save them. You knew them, didn't you?

In April 1945 you had all decided together to keep the city bridge from being blown up, you were all caught together, and together you were sentenced to death before a military tribunal—right?

But on the morning of the execution you were not taken from your cell together; instead, Chaplain Schorr, a man you hardly knew, went in your place. And you didn't ask why, you just let it happen?

You say you were sleeping?

You heard the firing squad shoot?

You sat up on your cot and looked around; the others were gone, including the Chaplain. You were alone, and you knew what the shots meant. Haven't those shots been ringing in your ears all this time, even now?

How have you been able to exist for thirty-five years knowing that you aren't really living your own life, but someone else's?

More to the point: how have you managed to live thirty-five years without knowing?

Mommsen says: I'm very thankful.

You haven't thought about what it means to have a stranger to thank for your life?

You've never thought about who this man is?

Thought about what might have made him choose you?

You wouldn't have thought about all this even now if it weren't for the fact that this man is being honored today for sacrificing his life?

And if Chaplain Schorr were suddenly standing in front of you and asked: I gave you thirty-five years and what have you done with them? How would you answer him?

Mommsen says: I'm very thankful, but—

You've simply attributed this event to your good fortune and left it at that? You haven't really tried in some way to live up to it?

And you consider yourself a happy man? Simply because you've been given a comfortable life?

You say you sleep soundly and don't have any dreams?

How do you do it?

You Shouldn't Have Been Afraid

All over, Nina said. You see, it's all over, and maybe it was a little confusing for you, but it really wasn't all that bad.

Nina is Mommsen's wife of twenty-two years; she knows him.

You were so afraid, she said, I'd like to know why. As if you needed to worry! Even your embarrassment there on the podium while the bishop gave his speech, and the mayor! You should've been proud. Think about how they must have felt, the church committee and the city council, when they found your name but didn't know who you were; the relief when they met you! This man could've been a real loser, this man the chaplain saved, a bum, a no-account, and they couldn't have done a thing, the celebration was set, and they'd have had to go ahead with this man, at least announce his name, the press would've found out everything.

But you were spooked, even at breakfast in the hotel when the two men came to pick you up. You tensed up, I saw you.

As if you were being arrested! And afterwards with the reporters you just mumbled; you stood there as if you were on trial.

You've probably buried it all inside, the shock of it all, and it's just now coming back to the surface. They have no right to do this to you.

Just look at the papers, they've all got your story. About how you worked your way up from practically nothing. " . . . and is today co-owner of a successful real estate firm . . ." You're my husband and I'm proud of you; I won't let you belittle yourself, not even in front of this chaplain.

Nina's observant eye, her constant watchfulness: How is he? Is he happy, moody, depressed? Did he have a bad dream? And where did these dreams come from? As she sends countless tiny sensors into his person, measuring brainwaves, heartbeat and circulation, combining the results with the sound of his voice, the color of his skin, the speed of his movements, with the level of his overall well-being, and comparing this with how he was yesterday, a speedy microprocessor making a judgment, and then, merely in passing, at the dinner table, raises her eyes: you're still a little upset, it'll be all right.

It'll be all right. She is a warm-hearted woman, he doesn't know what he'd do without her. She knows him better than he knows himself. He let himself stumble, she caught him.

The Monument

Newspapers, newspapers. They're all reporting the deed. The deed looms up like a cliff, crowned and made into a monument, Chaplain Schorr's heroic deed of thirty-five years ago, unlikely ever to be forgotten.

Mommsen's picture everywhere: humbly smiling, holding his hat in his hand, an embarrassed beneficiary standing there next to the lectern, very alone, as if left behind; helpless in the face of virtue. The caption reads: "A Lucky Man."

Next to his, again and again, the chaplain's face, quiet and kindly. Concerned, but unconcerned, as if he wanted to say: Dying is bad, but not all that bad; there are worse things than dying. Like having to watch someone else die, that's worse.

His large, dark eyes protrude slightly, wanting to reach out to anyone within their gaze, supporting. In this case: Mommsen.

It will be his companion from now on, assuming a face can be a companion, but there's nothing more than this face, and it will suffice completely.

Be Congratulated

From all sides: sympathy. People write him letters and they come up to him:

. . . may we offer you our most heartfelt congratulations! You have been chosen, you have—

Let me shake your hand! Where I come from, we believe it's good luck to touch a lucky person.

Well, you've been living here in our neighborhood for such a long time, and we didn't have the slightest idea you were such a famous man!

. . . just wanted to ask you for your autograph, for my grandson; he's an apprentice at a greenhouse, and all he wants is autographs and more autographs . . .

Saw you on the evening news: I'll be damned, I said to my wife, if that isn't Mommsen! What's that, she says, only half listening, has he gone into politics?

All these well-wishers, says Nina, and they're all so sincere. Really, it's quite amazing: a man is given the most valuable gift there is and no one envies him for it. Not like winning the lottery, or a new car, or a promotion . . . Then again, maybe it's not so surprising: Why should they envy you something they all have themselves?

Unfortunately He's Not a Cripple

Mommsen, the object of admiration, is wearing a plaid jacket, a coarse pattern but subtle colors, underneath that a turtleneck sweater made of pure cashmere, and he's had a manicure. He's left his coat unbuttoned.

You really look good! Nina says.

Too good. It's easy to get weary of this superficial harmony. If only he were a hunchback! That's it, Mommsen's gentle, sheeplike face on a deformed body, not letting him forget for one moment, forcing him constantly to fight to bring this natural dissonance to rest and order, Mommsen with a hunchback—even if it were just the hint of a hunchback, the kind any good tailor could hide! Someone like that would have more intensity in the tip of his little finger at any moment of the day than the well-formed Mommsen has deep in his heart in his most impassioned moments.

But Mommsen has grown straight and tall, and the hunchback he doesn't have on the outside has in some mysterious way grown inward, a tumor of conceit and selfishness, the insipid ballast of an untried soul.

Still, people like him. It's the kind of character he has; you can rely on certain appropriate responses. What is even better: he does not involve them, or at least no more than we normally involve each other—minimally. Others may be touched by his fate, why not, people allow themselves to be touched by things; out of gratitude that it's not them. If he's unlucky, then that's his business. After all, his good fortune back then, that was his business too. This is what makes him so likable.

Who's Talking?

Who's this talking here anyway? A dead priest? An inner voice? Or two, or three?—I don't want, says Mommsen, to be bothered with such trivial things.

That Was So Long Ago

The daily papers are there but not the weeklies and the monthlies, the questions continue, Mommsen hears them over the sounds of life around him, the dozens of greetings: Good morning! Good day! and Good evening! What was it like then? What was it like to be so close to death? What was it like, this newfound life?

Day in and day out it's a matter of life and death.

He'd like to get on with his business, he'd like everything to be the way it's been up till now, but they won't allow it, they force him to stop and think:

I can only say how thankful I am.

I don't know why. I don't know why he happened to choose me.

I was speechless; shaken. Completely overwhelmed.

The difference between him and us? We were afraid of death, and he wasn't, that was the difference.

I can't remember the details, I can't remember being afraid either.
It was such a long time ago, it's just not real to me any more.

You might ask what is real.

His work fulfills him, his days are laid out, meals, leisure. He has a loving wife. His house is big, his garden green . . .

He's let himself be crumbled up and dropped into this colorless soup, and because it's warm and moist, he feels good there.

Crumbs, that's a good word, comes from the time the peasant woman broke black bread into a large bowl and everyone took a spoon and—

His grandmother was a farmer's wife, she wore a scarf with fringes—small, stooped over, nimble, with a mouth like a monstrance, a radiance of wrinkles—the perfect image of a grandmother.

When she was done cooking and had washed the dishes and wiped the counters, she sat down in her rocking chair, smiling. Every evening she told her grandson a fairy tale, smoothed out his quilt and drew a cross on his forehead with her thumb. Then she went over to her own bed on the other side of the room, took off her scarf, pulled five pins from her hair and let a thin braid fall down her back, climbed out of her skirt and into bed, sighed and murmured: Sleep, my angel. Because during their shared summers Mommsen was her angel. What a vision! What a wonderful delusion! It was the high point of his life.

That was a long time ago but it is still real.

Froehlich Takes Notes

A reporter needs elbows to be successful. If he doesn't have elbows, then he should be as fragile, as blond, and as feckless as Froehlich. He'll get just as far that way, maybe further.

When Froehlich is excited he gets muddled. Then Mommsen answers before the question is completed, simply to put an end to the pain of formulation. And Froehlich takes copious notes.

You grew up in the country, isn't that so. Your father was a veterinarian, if I'm not mistaken.

He had a bad temper. When he got into a rage, he tore the door off its hinges and threw it into the room. Once he bit a horse that had knocked him down after he had pulled a painful nail out of its hoof. He didn't break the skin but it did him good; he said, there, you lout, you're lucky you've got such a thick skin.

When I was eight he hit me on the head so hard that I was

deaf for a week, and he yelled: now maybe you'll listen to me, you little bastard! Then he cried and we comforted him, my mother and I. We said: don't cry, it's not all that bad, the ear will get better, and it did get better, we can put the door back on its hinges, who needs doors anyway . . . And all of us, we all love you no matter what you do, we're not even mad at you, on the contrary we want you to be happy . . . And we really did want him to be happy. He was a work of nature and he was our responsibility.

He would have given his life for us and we knew it.

I think this man, in all his bad temper, was the right father for you. It's my theory, says Froehlich, that in your life you've always been lucky. You can see that in the way you came to your profession, without training, half finished with your economics major, it was more or less dumb luck. You had just transferred to a new university and you were looking for a place to stay—

A Cold Room

He was looking for a place to stay. It was fall and he rode his bicycle through the old residential quarter of the city, over red, yellow maple leaves, past rotting fences that protected run-down old houses. He had an image in his mind, and whenever he found a house that resembled this image he stopped and got off his bicycle, rang the bell and asked for an attic room.

It wasn't easy. Attic rooms were uninhabitable in the winter, sometimes there were windows missing or the roof leaked, and if they were habitable they were already occupied.

Doctor Bernsdorff, a retired doctor, who lived with his sister in a villa with many turrets, said: there's no water and no toilet up there, for that you have to run down three flights of stairs to the basement. And besides it's very cold in those garrets, you might just as well sleep on the street. You'll get a chronic sinus infection; you had better take your aspirin right with your dinner.

Mommsen moved in. He froze but he didn't get sick. In the evenings he warmed himself at Doctor Bernsdorff's tile stove. My grandfather built this house, said the doctor, my father grew up here, I grew up here, my son grew up here. But if you find me a three-room apartment with central heating and hot running water, you can have this castle for a song.

Doctor Bernsdorff's sister, standing behind his chair chewing on her fingernails, which gave her the appearance of a seventy-year-old child, said: Doctor Bernsdorff's son died at Stalingrad.

I can name you a half dozen people in similar circumstances, said Doctor Bernsdorff.

Lucky Again

Well, that was the beginning. He dropped out of the university and took a job as a real estate agent. He wasn't shrewd nor was he a particularly good businessman, he was simply attracted to certain houses, and once again he was lucky: it was his time. His customers trusted his advice, they sensed that he really did love the houses he was praising and they began to see those houses through his eyes, they bought his dreams.

He could have become very wealthy, he settled for well-to-do. He was never greedy.

If he counts up all the houses he has sold or brokered in twenty years he could build a small city, not a particularly organic one since there is no church nor city hall nor any other public building, but it is pleasantly full of turn-of-the-century villas with their turrets and overgrown gardens, and a few townhouses, which surprisingly enough do not detract, they are covered with vines and surrounded by young trees, small pyramid forests partitioned by colorful awnings. He's pleased with his city, he'd be happy to live there.

You are a fortunate man. And you've never really stopped to think?

You forget that I'm just an ordinary man. I am thankful for every moment; if it's a beautiful day I feel good. Admittedly it doesn't take much; it's enough if I get hungry, or thirsty, or tired, then I can eat, drink, and sleep. Things are just that simple.

Be that as it may, says Froehlich, we have to have at least a minimum of biographical content; everyone's got some biography. If you could give us just the slightest bit of help . . .

Mommsen wants to be helpful. Still he just can't seem to discover a chronology in the course of his life. He looks back on a mass of biographical data, a number of more or less significant contacts, a swatch of war experiences that now seem more like an excerpt from an old newsreel, everything vaguely familiar . . . And, of course, a chain of events that never really happened: lost opportunities.

For example?

That trip to Agerswihl. That's already more that twenty years ago, it was just after we were married. I wanted to show my wife the prison and ask about the priest, maybe visit his grave. But then I saw the vineyards again.

The vineyards?

Just as they were then, the tightly framed view from a barred window: out onto leafless vineyards, stem upon stem, thousands of planted rifles, a monstrous graveyard full of half-finished crosses. A manipulated landscape. Not one inch left uncultivated, not one stone untouched. And geometry everywhere, rectangles, rhomboids, trapezoids, pole upon pole, inbetween pole crossing pole, cross, cross, fallen in the year.

And now the inn.

I had wanted to show Nina everything, but I didn't show her anything, I just said: I was here once during the war. Then we drove off.

I understand, says Froehlich.

Why Vineyards?

Nina says: Vineyards? Why vineyards? For her Agerswihl was the last stop on her honeymoon trip, mainly that.

When they arrived, everything was still possible. The prison was in the middle of town; they walked on past the wall, which was dusty with chipping paint during the war but now had a fresh coat of yellow. Mommsen said: Tomorrow. Tomorrow we'll go inside and then I'll tell you everything. After that they said nothing. They didn't talk very much at all those days, there was no need to say very much.

Later they went to the inn. Having been given a table in the middle of the dining room, they sat down and reached for the menu. They didn't look up at each other, they hardly even exchanged a smile, rather they seemed to be smiling to themselves, and when they talked it was in hushed tones, merely incidental. The waiter came and asked for their order, which he repeated after them with quiet enthusiasm. They thanked him and said nothing further. Quiet radiated out from their table in concentric circles. Guests leaned back in their chairs, some playing thoughtfully with their forks, others twirling their glasses by the stems. Against a backdrop of wood stood the innkeeper's wife wearing a cobalt blue dress, between fruit and cheese. The light from the table lamps deepened, the outside noise ebbed away into silence. Wine lay mellow in the glass.

The yellow wall was there in the morning, Mommsen saw it from his window, but he still said nothing. Instead he pulled the curtains closed and ordered breakfast. Nina answered the knock at the door, took the breakfast tray from the maid and waited until the door closed again. Mommsen observed this and thanked her, they smiled at each other.

You don't want to show me the prison at all, said Nina, you just want us to go home.

You're right, Mommsen said, let's go home.

Now it all comes back to me: You never really told me, Nina says, about the chaplain, and that he died for you.

Your Precious Existence!

She is kneeling on the floor; in front of her, all around her she has laid out articles and pictures from newspapers, a chaotic jumble, it seems to him at first, yet after his initial surprise he can see that she has arranged the papers in the form of a large "M." A photograph of the priest used as a period.

He bends over, touches her hair, waits for a response, turns away when none is forthcoming, turns back and looks into her upturned face, waits for a smile, sighs when there is no smile, and for a long time this sigh seems to him to be the only sound in his empty house.

You said there were four of you sentenced to death and that the priest sacrificed himself for all of you. You didn't tell me you were the only one he saved and that the others had to die.

You misunderstood; he was only able to save one of us, that was all. Besides, I don't see why this has occurred to you just now, or what difference it makes anyway.

You don't see why? That is the difference. You're not just one person in a group of people who was lucky, no: you were the only one, the chosen one, your life seemed so precious to another man that he sacrificed his own for yours. Your precious existence!

I didn't ask him to die for me.

But if you had been able to ask him, you would have.

Yes, I would have. What would you have done?

Nothing like this would ever happen to me. There are only those very few, people like you, who have ever had anything like this happen to them.

Nina picks up one of the pages from the carpet, it is the

usual photo of Mommsen standing next to the lectern, he has seen it often enough, but this time he sees it through Nina's eyes: the guilt-ridden man, the poor sinner. A bank robber who has been living on stolen millions for years; now they are dragging him out into the open, and what's more: they are forcing him to ask himself if it has really been worth it.

The light in this photograph is unforgiving; Mommsen knows it is coming from the picture window in his bungalow, from the rounded-off edges, the ice blue walls, the circulating air. This is not a house, this is an aquarium.

Mommsen asks himself how he ever came to live in an edifice that so obviously conflicts with his tastes. He knows there were good reasons, but he cannot remember any of them. Maybe it was just this contrast, the desire to broaden his all-too-narrow horizons, to escape from earlier images? And, of course, to please Nina. Nina hates the old boxes he sells for a living.

Now they look around and cannot find their footing, slipping and sliding wherever they turn. And it is just this they have spent years, even decades, achieving: burnishing and polishing, fine-tuning. They are like glass in glass, no impurities, no cracks; around them consonance and quiet.

Mommsen has nothing to hold on to. He would like to settle in.

Homesick at Home

This is a sickness he has carried with him from childhood: homesickness for the place he is at; the inability to truly be where he is. Yearning for distant places is a lesser evil, he can still hope that travel to those places may help. But for homesickness at home, there is no cure.

Mostly he has yearned for houses he has seen on trips, houses which somehow seemed familiar to him. Once it was a small villa in a town in Italy, once it was a grand castle of a house with gables and turrets standing next to an empty factory, once it was a stone cube in the glaring sunlight somewhere on a southern coast. They all exuded familiarity, they all confounded him with their challenge: why don't you live here? It was hard for him simply to walk by.

Just once he lived in one of those houses, that was the year they built their bungalow. They had leased the broken-down building near their new property; since the turn of the century it had been a café in the forest, the innkeeper's heirs had barely maintained it; when subdivisions had edged ever nearer, finally surrounding the house, they sold the land for a high price to a condominium developer who then leased the house to Mommsen until the start-up of construction.

Barely a year, not more. But what a year! For the first time since those days spent with his grandmother he was at home where he lived. He walked across the creaky floors, puttied up the leaky windows on the veranda, he spent long hours in this glassed-in cage which contained nothing but a forgotten rocking chair and a faded rug, sitting there awaiting dusk; he was happy.

Nina said she couldn't take living in this barn for a whole year. She fixed up the kitchen and the bedroom on the second floor as best she could, and ignored the rest of the house. I could live my life here, Mommsen said; without me, Nina said.

He called it "the old house" as if he had always lived there.

The bathroom was as big as a living room, the water heater burned logs, there were wicker chairs, rag rugs covered the floor, the tub had claws, the curtain which hung over the window was made of a cotton print, brown medicine bottles lined the shelf, the mirror was half clouded over and framed in gold.

He had always wanted a house like this, and now he had it. He had it for a short time and then never again. All his life he will have to be homesick for a house that stood five minutes away from his own, but is no longer there.

Sometimes, in the old house, when he went through the main room on the ground floor where there was a dusty old Ping-Pong table, ribbons of light shining through the jalousie windows conjured up a similar table, a dining table for twelve, set with a white table cloth, flowers, plates, a steaming tureen . . . For a large family with children, young people, old people, happy people . . . Who knew where they belonged: at the stroke of one at this table, for example, and in their gabled rooms under wood and shingles on which they heard the rain pattering. Where it smelled of hay and pine, and snow, of roasts in the oven, of wood burning in the fireplace, of dreams and fantasies and music.

He should have been one of them, but he never was. He wondered if they had noticed: he knew they had missed him from time to time, or at least sensed his absence. But they had

only looked up briefly and then turned back to the ones who
were seated there.

The Trunk

The new stillness is hard to take, not just for him, as
Mommsen notes when Nina tells him she has invited guests.
She wants to fill the empty rooms, that's fine with him.

Basically he hates socializing. As a child he used to hide in a
trunk in the attic when guests came to visit. He felt so protected there that his sense of security even carried over to times
when he was forced to shake hands with strangers in the street,
all he had to do was think about his trunk to feel safe, as if protected by some invisible shield.

Until one evening when his mother in her breathless voice
made him promise never, ever, ever, ever to climb into a box or
a trunk. Even before the boy could claim, with a dissembling
smile, that he had never, even in his dreams, considered doing
such a thing, his mother began reading aloud from the local
paper, a terrible story of two young girls who had suffocated in
a chest because the lock had shut and could not be opened

from the inside. They were found by chance, clasped tightly in each other's arms, weeks after the entire area had been searched with police dogs . . .

An ordinary chest with a spring lock! cried the mother. The father asked: Do we have anything like that? We certainly wouldn't have anything like that!—But now the young son weakens and says: But we do! And with a cry the mother leaps up from the table, on up the steps, into the attic. She opens the chest, lets the top fall, and the lock snaps shut; it never snapped shut when Mommsen was in the chest, but only because he had closed it so gently. Crying and laughing the mother takes the chalk pale son into her arms.

From now on the young Mommsen sleeps fitfully. He dreams that he is trapped in the trunk, sometimes alone, sometimes together with the two little girls, and bathed in sweat he wakes up from the sound of his own scream. He has just turned eleven and now politely greets any visiting guest: he has seen how terribly flight is punished, and he knows how very lucky he was to have gotten away with it.

But the shyness is still there; when he has to face a number of people at one time, he still wants to creep away. Screams inside himself loud enough to mask other voices. Screams and more screams.

Why do you look that way?

What way?

So—strained.

Yelling is stressful. But yelling also creates quiet, it makes others stop talking.

Aren't you listening at all?

I'm listening. Yes.

Who's Barking?

Did you hear that barking? When did the Mommsens get a dog?

That's not Mommsen's dog, that's Pavlov's dog.

He's trained: When he hears a bell he gets hungry. Even if it's not time to eat. His stomach growls and he slobbers.

Ring and slobber, that's charming.

When Kurt sits down at the breakfast table he has to have the morning paper; if the day's paper has not yet been delivered, he reads an old one. He does not need a paper when he is sitting on the sofa.

So what. I don't give a damn about the dog; he can get hungry whenever he wants.

But he doesn't get hungry whenever he wants, he gets hungry when he hears the bell.

Dogs don't think. I think but I don't slobber. Though I'll have to admit: when I come home and see Ingrid in her apron at the door, I do salivate . . .

You never used to think about eating when you came home.

You never used to cook that well.

Whenever Eduard sees a mountain hut he gets thirsty.

Kurt gets thirsty even without seeing a mountain hut.

When Ingrid senses spring in the air, she has to clean the house; from top to bottom, it's like a curse.

Not one of us can change his stripes.

I don't even want to, I feel fine just the way I am; don't you?

Besides, there's nothing so enduring as a really good, well-ingrained habit: you save your feelings and live on the interest . . .

A little kiss in the morning, a little kiss in the evening, even after twenty years. Stable relationships, an orderly existence.
Mommsen never wanted things any different.

From cradle to grave—ring and slobber.

That is why time passes so quickly as you get older. Before we know it we become automatons. Everything happens automatically and we do not even realize it. No more independent decisions possible. What gets lowered into the grave is a machine.

I think you're taking this much too seriously.

After all it's only a game.

Nina in the Garden

The house is now emptier than before, their steps are even softer on the carpet, they glide toward one another, past one another, along seemingly endless stretches, they exchange polite words, meet in the bedroom, in one bed that is big enough for two individual sleepers, and meet during the day at the dinner table where meals are eaten.

For the first time it occurs to Mommsen that it would be nice to have a dog.

It is the end of May and already very warm, Nina is spending a lot of time in the garden, at first she works a little with the flowers but then she just sits there.

She is wearing a white dress and a straw hat, and there's a book lying on her knees. That is how she sits in the sun, hour after hour, without looking up. Half a day goes by before he notices that she has not turned a page.

What are you doing with that book if you're not reading it?

I need it.

Then he sees what she is doing: she is holding her diamond ring so that the reflected light dances across the printed letters, creating a cosmos of suns and planets, shafts of rainbow color in between, everything in gentle circling motion—

He had given her the ring on their wedding day.

Sometimes I don't understand you.

She says: please go away, and he goes, turns around once as he's going and sees that she's already forgotten him.

Nina at lunch appears to have no appetite, she puts her fork down, rests her elbow on the arm of her chair, lets her hand fall from her wrist and leans her head to the side to observe it: object transparent, she says.

The flies are more annoying than usual, they crawl over Nina's hands, disperse lazily when they are brushed away, wander over her ears and neck into the collar of her dress, get trapped buzzing in her hair, until Mommsen can no longer bear watching and, letting out a yell, leaps at her.

She stares at him until all he can do is mumble excuses: I've never seen flies that crawl over a person as if—he wants to say—as if crawling over a cadaver, but that is not what he says, instead object is the word he uses, and Nina looks at her arm where a fly, having just been chased away, has already returned, and says: We all think ourselves so terribly alive, don't we?

These days she often brings rocks home, lays them out in front of her and stares at them until, from a seemingly form-less surface, arteries and fissures appear, landscapes and faces. Under a yew tree in the garden she has laid out flat stones to form a mosaic, sometimes she kneels in front of it and reads it like a picture book. At first Mommsen admires her patience but then it begins to frighten him.

This is the time when she begins to read everything, stars, cards, coffee grounds. Just as she used to search his face: what is happening there, how will it affect me? He doesn't know what she sees.

As Mommsen opens the house door in the evening, he

hears Nina talking. He goes in and looks around:

No one's here!

I'm here, Nina says.

But you were talking . . .

When someone's alone he can sing or cough, that's all. The moment he begins to laugh or talk, he's crazy. I've sung enough and coughed enough, she says, I don't want to sing and cough anymore.

Mommsen believes she is crazy.

Still he cautiously tries appealing to her reason:

It's just that there's a danger you'll distance yourself too far from reality . . . And Nina, in her polite new tone that raises goose bumps along his spine:

Which reality are you talking about? Yours?

Tea with Froehlich

Work still helps, it is just the weekends he dreads. With a sense of relief he agrees to meet Froehlich between three and four on Saturday afternoon.

But between three and four Mommsen is still with a client, Nina is alone. She leads Froehlich into the living room, she shows the room: Charming, isn't it? Then, in a confidential tone: Just between the two of us, this isn't going to last.

Froehlich is amazed; he knows her only as a wife whose sole concern is Mommsen's well-being.

Would you like a sherry? And Froehlich watches her walk, first straight through the living room and then diagonally across it, even though the sherry and the glasses are in the bar cupboard behind her back. Still, what Nina is doing seems to be what must be done.

Of course you're waiting for my husband, she says, and I'm

sure he'll be here right away. She sits down on the edge of the sofa across from Froehlich.

Naturally you don't like him, she says; you should put yourself in his shoes, but you don't want to put yourself in his shoes, you don't like him well enough. I can easily understand that. He's slick, too modest, which is always a sign of arrogance, don't you think, a man with a polished surface. He lets you slide off him like a drop of water: 'I'm afraid there isn't much I can do for you, nothing really, what you see here is an ordinary man, the ordinary man . . . ' You'd have to grab on to him with grappling hooks to get close, don't you see?

Froehlich believes there is something to what Nina is saying, just that she's exaggerating a little.

All I need now is a few biographical details.

Oh that, the thing about the children.

The children?

You wrote about that yourself, Nina says.

She stands up and goes to a cupboard, this time without

taking a detour, she comes back with a packet of newspapers and finds what she wants immediately: "There is really no longer any doubt: the chaplain sacrificed his life for the life of a father. Whether he mistook the soldier Mommsen for a father, or simply believed Mommsen would become one—it is the only credible motive. A deed, we might say, dedicated to the survival of humankind . . ."

I wrote that, Froehlich says, but what I was thinking—

You were thinking about Richard and Viktoria. Richard would now be nineteen, and Viktoria seventeen. We had already chosen the names. The first child was going to be a boy and the second a girl; like most families. Richard would have been born in December, a Sagittarius; the following January my husband joined the firm. Two years after that we built our house; Viktoria would have been an Aries, stubborn, strong-willed. A Sagittarius and an Aries—they would have gotten along so well.

Froehlich clears his throat.

I know, Nina says, this isn't what you're looking for. You're only interested in guilt. As far as that goes: he won't ever live long enough to make up for that.

At this juncture Mommsen arrives home.

I was just telling Mr. Froehlich about our children, about how we traded them for your career and for the house.

My wife hasn't been feeling very well these days, Mommsen says.

Oh, but there's where you're wrong, I feel just fine!

Maybe I should come some other time, Froehlich says.

Please stay! Mommsen says.

Yes, please do stay, Nina says, I'll go make us some tea.

At the door to the kitchen she turns around:

Mr. Froehlich is having some problems with his article. Being trapped won't make a story, unless of course it turns out to have been an illusion.

I hope you'll understand, Mommsen says. He now has a glass in his hand and is walking back and forth with it in front of the picture window. Nina is ill; this thing with the priest has affected her more than it has me.

Do you think so?

Children! Mommsen says, as if that were ever a problem! Back then we agreed completely, Nina and I, I didn't try to influence her, I didn't put her in a situation where she had no options. If I had said: good, have a baby and just see where we get the money to pay the rent—but that wasn't the problem, not at all, it's just that we'd made plans, for the following year, for what we were going to spend—

We said: we'll have to discuss this and then we discussed it and decided against it, the way it happens everyday in countless households, family planning, right. We planned to have children later, we said: now while we're getting established, we wouldn't really have time for a child, our child would have things a lot better once we were settled. That happened once and then again and then we just didn't talk about it anymore, not for years. Then we knew Nina was no longer able to have children. We talked about that once in a hospital room, briefly, with some regret, as if we were giving up on some cherished hope, with a shrug of the shoulders: it just wasn't meant to be.

Nina brings the tea. She talks about the weather: sometimes this severe heat makes us sad and then sometimes it makes us happy; you just can't count on a summer like this.

Finally Froehlich is able to take his leave.

The Excursion

Getting Nina to the psychiatric clinic for evaluation is easier than he could have hoped:

Of course it's a good idea! I'd be interested myself to see what comes of it. We can never know, can we? Besides, it'll do me good to get out of the house for a few days.

The clinic is in a park, Mommsen leaves the car at the gate, they walk the rest of the way in. There must have been a heavy rain here, the ground is soft, Nina in her open sandals searches for firm footing.

They have an encounter at the front door: a patient is standing there, formless in a raincoat and rubber boots, dull gray hair and a face like a worn coin. Mommsen flinches, while Nina seems hardly to notice.

The patient is trusting, she looks Nina over from head to toe, compares her own boots with Nina's delicate sandals, looks at the muddy path and taps her finger to her forehead.

Nina laughs.

Mommsen does not understand why her laugh is so surprising, but when the door opens for them and he enters the clinic behind the two patients, he suddenly realizes it is senseless to bring Nina here, she does not need it anymore than he does.

And just that, in carefully chosen words, is what the doctor says when Mommsen returns five days later to pick up his wife. But still he shouldn't feel bad about it. These days in the clinic were certainly not wasted; and Nina seems to have enjoyed her stay.

Her bag is packed, but Nina is not in her room; Nina is in the kitchen.

The cook is standing at the stove whisking a sauce over a double-boiler. From time to time he looks up at Nina. Nina is standing with her arms folded, leaning against the dishwasher and watching the cook. The cook looks young and innocent, self-assured, chaste. He looks like Mommsen looked twenty-two years ago.

Nina's lips are slightly parted. The cook looks up and then back down. It is very quiet in the kitchen, the rest of the staff has left, a dripping faucet measures out the time, the refrigerator drones on.

Nina breaks off her gaze and lets her eyes follow the line of his half-open lips down to his chin and his jacket, down to the burner with the double boiler.

The cook gives a start and checks the sauce, it is almost finished. He is beating it very hard now while his eyes follow Nina, who with still-folded arms pushes herself away from the dishwasher and slowly turns to go through an open door into the pantry where she takes a bottle from the shelf, grabs a glass, fills it halfway, turns slowly back around, drinks.

She looks past the rim of the glass at the cook, who finally takes the sauce off the burner, puts the whisk and the double boiler into the sink, dries his hands; and who, his cheeks flushed from a quickened pulse and from Nina's smile that surrounds him like a liquid, warm and moist, looks like Mommsen when he was young.

There is no question the sauce was left on the stove too long, it's overcooked, pungent and salty, not spoiled, not that, but an essence.

Why Are You So Surprised?

He will remember the trip home.

Nina is well again, more precisely she has been well all along, she simply had a brief episode of unusual behavior, that is not uncommon, the doctor says, it may even recur, it is merely a sign that something is working itself out and that she is continuing to develop emotionally.

You're surprised, Nina says, why are you so surprised? Did you think I had lost my mind? But my dear, she says, I'm not crazy! I was mistaken, that's all: I created a vision of what I wanted you to be. I mistook weak for gentle.

And now?

Now it's time we scraped off the sugar coating to see what's underneath.

Sugar coating!

I've started to wonder. When I see the way you squirm and look for an escape, the way you still hope you can survive this—how, how in the world?—then I ask myself: did the priest really know he was doing good when he let himself be shot to save you, or did he just think he was? After all we should see what is good by the fruits of our deeds, and the fruit of his deed, that would have to be, after so many years, you, here, today, you, in front of my eyes—

Okay, good, Mommsen says, but is all this hostility really necessary?

Apparently, Nina says, apparently.

Mommsen thinks that it had not seemed so necessary before, then he thinks back and finds that from the beginning it always was one of Nina's possible modes.

They met on a bus on a windy day in March. Nina, at the end of the line, leapt up, crumpled her newspaper together, threw it onto Mommsen's lap, and cried: there, take it! Or don't you read newspapers you have to hold in your own hands!

He stared at her; it had been a long time since anyone had yelled at him.

The bus stopped, the doors hissed open, Nina got out and walked down the street, Mommsen followed, the doors hissed shut, Nina stopped and turned around, Mommsen was startled, the bus drove away.

A damp wind blew across the square, a man in a loden coat was carrying his purchases home, a long broom and a carpetsweeper, Mommsen said: Mommsen.

She seemed young and spoiled, that's all. It was a long time before he noticed that she was someone distinct, it was not even evident on the first trip they took together until one day he saw her on the beach. He had come to pick her up for dinner, the other guests were already seated in the dining room, the sun was setting, he wanted to call out to her, but then he saw how she was kneeling in the sand and praying.

She was sitting on her heels letting her head rest on her folded hands, facing the sea at an angle to the sun. The leeward wind blew her hair from both sides over her shoulders into her face. Mommsen waited for what seemed a long time. As she let her hands fall, lifted her head, stood up and wiped the sand from her knees, fastened her robe and picked up her bag, he came up to her and thought: I'm going to marry her.

From that time on they were engaged, even though they never talked about it, and when they finally did talk, it was like a repetition of something that had been agreed upon for a long time.

It occurs to him now that he has not seen her pray since.

Weak or gentle, Nina says, you always were a total fool.

It Would Have Been So Simple

Mommsen dreams that the priest is crossing the prison yard and leaving unhindered through the gate, while the other four, himself included, are standing with their faces to the wall. The priest leaves without looking back, goes down the street and into a house where he takes off his uniform jacket and puts on a handknit sweater, all of a sudden he is surrounded by a family, apparently his own, a woman in a full skirt holding a child on one arm, three older children who call him "Father," he tells them to wash their hands before coming to the table, the children obey, the woman goes to the stove and stirs the pot, still holding the child on one arm, she carries the pot to the table, the children sit down on the bench, the father sits down, the mother sits down, the father crosses himself, they pray: "And forgive us our trespasses."

How cowardly, Nina says, to let yourself dream this kind of solution, nothing but an excuse! Pitiful!

It is Sunday, a restless morning, Nina is wandering around the house, it occurs to Mommsen that even her walk has changed, her stride is longer, almost belligerent. Sitting sunk down in his chair, his elbows resting on the upholstered arms, he follows her passage, back and forth, back and forth, while Nina speaks.

There you sit, she says: mute. All these questions they've been asking you and not one single answer. But that's just it: a life made up of marriage and career, that's it. No room for anything else. Sunk into the upholstery. The palest thought, the slightest impulse—swallowed up before it can emerge into the light. Nothing that can grow, ferment, build up, no highs no lows, a tepid bath, a hideous waste. Are you surprised?

Of course, it's not just you, it's me too. But my life is my life, I can do what I want with it. And even if I don't make anything of it, that's my business. But your case is different, right? Isn't that so?

We should have had children, Mommsen says.

It would have been so simple, he thinks; a house full of children, a full life. Or: we pile up a mountain of rocks in front of our door and make our lives useful by shoveling them away. Crazy! On the other hand: wasn't there a power dictating that there be a mountain of rocks in front of everyone's door? And: blessed is he who has many rocks to shovel? But what power is this? To what extent was it right?

If you really believe that children might provide your only justification, your alibi: why don't you get a divorce and start all over again? Or are you afraid that one day you'd find yourself standing there and realizing: not even children have made a difference, the void is still there—I've taken the easy way out?

Mommsen raises his hand from the arm of the chair and lets it fall again. This minimal gesture is too much for Nina. She stops and glares at him.

No, she says, of course not; you couldn't even manage that.

Trees Are Better

Mommsen now has an enemy in his house, a situation he had feared all his life, indeed he had not even dared imagine it. But now it has come to pass and amazingly enough: walls are not collapsing around his head and nothing has come to an end, it is just that he has been set adrift.

Suddenly he has time. He reads and goes for walks, usually on the narrow path along the old estates; he loves all kinds of fences, the crisscross fences made of wood, iron fences on stone footings, high fences with lance-sharp posts; the impermanent demarcation.

The following Sunday he drives to the woods. He parks his car among the raspberries and currant bushes near the edge of the road and takes a few steps into a stand of trees. There he stops, drops his head back and lets his arms hang loosely at his side. He neither sees the sunlight shining through the spruce trees nor hears the twitter of the birds announcing his arrival; he does not even smell the mushrooms or the pine sap, and just the mere accounting of these things could ruin the whole excursion for him. He does not think, he just stands there, but as he leaves the woods and climbs into his car he feels refreshed, renewed.

Trees give off energy. Bismarck's personal physician advised him to embrace an oak tree whenever he needed strength. Good advice, assuming one still has the strength to embrace an oak. Wouldn't another human being do as well? But trees are better: they don't run away when you need them, and if you yourself choose to go they don't follow.

Mommsen needs strength; he is determined to pull himself together, he pulls the outrunners of his person back into himself, his habits, diversions, the whirling thoughts. He is surprised at how easy this is and how little he misses.

He throws himself into his work. At exactly eight o'clock the next morning he is sitting in his office, collecting folders from filing cabinets, studying, taking notes, comparing, finding deals to be made. At midday he has sandwiches and coffee brought in, then he calls Jacobs, his assistant, and gives him instructions.

He meets with two clients one after another, both looking for upscale housing, one of them is living in an old apartment, the other has a rowhouse, they are both looking to improve their lot. Mommsen knows they are interested in fixtures for the most part, in garbage disposals, radiant heating, heated towel racks in the bathroom. Neither wants to build, one because he feels he is too old, the other because he has already built once and found it too trying. Mommsen resists the strong temptation to offer them his own house; thoughts of Nina keep him from doing this. Later, perhaps.

By the time his workday is over, in addition to completing his regular schedule, he has sold a new apartment house which had been on the market for months. He organizes his notes for the following day, things can go on this way.

They do go on for two days; on the third day as he is crossing the parking space of a condominium he has just sold, calculations swirling in his head, the spring of success in his step, he suddenly sees himself again: on the hundreds of parking spaces of his early years, with the same spring in his step, pushing relentlessly forward—on to a larger car, a larger condominium, a house.

There is nothing wrong here. It is just that all this has led nowhere, except to the very point he now finds himself.

Vanessa

There's not much going on at the office right now, Momm-sen says; we could go visit your mother.

I know about these visits, Nina says, a precaution: one day I'll be that old and I'll be happy to have someone visit, so I'll earn this visit by making one myself today.

Mathildenruh is situated over a ravine, water meanders along the bottom, a black stream where willows wade, while above, the gables of the retirement home are glistening through the tops of the beech trees, baroque ornamentation white as bones.

A hearse is racing up the hillside, speed having little to do with its task, the driver just wants to be done, he who steps on the gas is still alive.

I'm no fan of terminal phases, Nina says, I hate the fragrance of decay.

Vanessa is sitting in front of an open window wearing a man's suit, a hat pulled down over her face, resting her chin and her hand on her cane—a handsome old man, gnarled, leathery. Alone in a large room, surrounded by flora and images of flora: the tops of beech trees outside, roses on the rug, a monstrous philodendron covering half the wall.

All by yourself, Mama?

Not at all, Vanessa says, you underestimate the greenery. Philodendrons, for example, are very sensitive; a mean thought is enough to cause them distress, a pleasant thought to cheer them up. That's more than I've ever been able to accomplish in a human relationship.

It's been a long time since our last visit, Mommsen says.

My daughter has never cared much for people who are so much older than she is. I can understand that; of course she doesn't expect that they care much for her either.

No, Mama.
And Mommsen is certainly busy.

He's forever busy making himself feel guilty.

Nina's exaggerating, Mommsen says.

Guilt! Vanessa says, how tedious! How extraordinarily superfluous! Unhealthy, destructive! Always bringing guilt down on yourself: the curse of the egocentric, delusions of grandeur in reverse.

He can't bring himself to love his savior.

What a reproach! Loving is a talent. Let those with no talent feel guilty. Your poor savior! Why isn't he endearing enough to melt this stone?

Be that as it may, Nina says, Mommsen is suffering. And at the same time he despises anyone else who may be better off. Such arrogance, such conceit! When I think about who looks down upon whom and for what, I get sick.

My dear child, says Vanessa, let's not fool ourselves: that which unites us with our fellow man, besides the weather—'I believe it's getting cloudy, I believe it's clearing up'—it is after all our conceit. It may show up as class consciousness, an artist's pride, a believer's or a martyr's pride, but it always means the same thing: setting downward limits, because it's the very nature of conceit that there is nothing superior, at most something adjacent. How pleasant, how reassuring! Without conceit what would we be? We would be, heaven forbid, just like anyone else.

Furthermore, she says to Mommsen, your case is not really so exceptional: every war is full of noble deeds, friends sacrifice themselves for friends, captains for their companies, partisans for their villages . . . We don't know about most of them, sometimes even those who are saved don't know.

Just that they're all men. When has a man ever really sacrificed himself for a woman? When he jumps from a church steeple because of unrequited love: that's his love and not hers! And the hundreds upon hundreds who've dueled in the early morning mists, supposedly to defend the honor of a woman: what they really died for was their own pride and nothing else.

Mama's in good form today.

Only intellectually, Vanessa says.

She wants to get up; it is an excruciating process, a propping up, a stretching, and a shifting of weight. She turns down Mommsen's offer of help; she suppresses a groan.

Owing thanks! That sounds like a joke to me. Wasn't it

some sort of a deal? He saved your life, you saved him from aging. He might be sitting in a wheelchair today, with rheumatism, gout, arthritis. You may be sitting in a wheelchair twenty years from now!

She stands leaning on her cane, her fedora pulled down over her face, gnarled, callous, without a kind thought. Yellow, the whites of her blue eyes, looking off into the distance where they do not have to rest upon any human figure; bright in spite of all this.

If you do not want to become an old woman, you will have to become an old man.

The Good Deed

The visit to Vanessa has shown Mommsen that he can expect no outside help; he now carries the foolish look of a man committed to do good, cost what it may, no matter what the consequences. He has the ponderous look of a frustrated philanthropist: the world is full of suffering, right? But where to begin.

He increases his contributions to good causes, doubling them in some cases, but this brings very little satisfaction: the goal is certainly praiseworthy, but the contribution is too limited, the sums hardly show up at all in his bank statement, and the fact that he can deduct them from his taxes is just one more proof that what he is doing is no more than what is expected of any man.

Since he no longer spends his evenings with Nina he has time to look around. These days, on the way home from the office, he makes a detour through the suburbs and the poorer parts of town, drinks a beer here and a beer there and keeps his eyes open.

He does not find any dire need; he finds trivial, everyday worries, illness, bills, the kind of things he himself might be bothered with, just on a somewhat more elevated plane.

When he finally finds a victim, it is not in the poorer neighborhoods, but in the area around the central train station which is also the red-light district, and it comes to pass with such banality that he has the feeling he has already read about it in a mystery or seen it played out in the movies: the street flooded with the harsh glare of neon lights, the crush of traffic, the door to the nightclub illuminated in red, the door opens, letting noise, music and a man escape, he is holding onto a woman's collar with his left hand and hitting her across the face with his right.

Mommsen, who has just accompanied an out-of-town client to his hotel, draws back in disgust; he hails an approaching taxi, opens the door. There is nothing else to it, the woman has been rescued, she is sitting next to him in the taxi, hair dyed blonde, made up, very ordinary, she touches her face and thanks him. Mommsen forces himself to listen to her story.

She talks at great length about the man who has brought her to such unfortunate circumstances, how jealous he is, how brutal . . . He hit her whenever he felt like it, he never considered marrying her, he spent his money on himself and at times he even pocketed some of her earnings . . . But she'll show him, she'd like to see his face when they pull her out of the water and lay her at his front door . . . It's the reason she carries a slip of paper with his name and address on it.

Mommsen has difficulty hiding his antipathy. She has robbed him of any sense of satisfaction he might have felt for having rescued her. He's relieved when he finally sees her eating, a full dinner with two desserts, it keeps her quiet.

Of course she can't go back to her apartment because the brute is lying in wait for her, she doesn't want to go to a shelter for battered women either, she's been there so often they won't take her in anymore, she says. Mommsen suggests a hotel, thankful that she thankfully agrees, for a brief moment he finds her tolerable, almost attractive, images burst into his mind, making him uneasy: rescuer and rescued in the glow of a bedside lamp, much flesh, a little too pink for his taste—

Mommsen gets hold of himself; he won't even consider sacrificing this good deed, so painstakingly accomplished, for the much more easily sated weaknesses of the flesh, he resists. Satisfied with this victory, he pays the restaurant check and later he pays an unexpectedly high price for a room with breakfast in an unassuming little hotel in the suburbs. He even remembers to pick up a toothbrush and soap, the needs of his guest have been met, the rescue appears complete.

Shortly thereafter, in a narrow vestibule, a pink-shaded bulb the only touch of luxury, the illusion melts making way for the nightmare, its contours all the sharper by comparison: Mommsen on the lower step of the hotel stairs, his hand extended in a gesture of leave-taking; the rescued woman three steps above him in her cheap coat, the room key with its heavy wooden fob in her hand, while in quick succession her expression changes: bewilderment, disbelief, incomprehension, and finally the wounded realization, the sulking hurt of one rejected.

As he steps into the street, the porter's puzzled look at his back and a bitter taste in his mouth, it occurs to him that he does not even know her name.

The Pancakes

Why do we need such a big house? he asks Nina at breakfast, and Nina looks at him attentively and says: We don't need it, we want it so we don't feel cramped for space. But Mommsen feels himself surrounded by rooms that have no other purpose than to shelter his and Nina's vast possessions, wooden things used to hold things made of cloth, leather, paper, silver and porcelain, multiples of every piece, it would be enough for ten people to wear, use, read . . . What gaps are they meant to fill, what deficiencies to mask?

Strange thoughts, Nina says, for a real estate agent.

While he continues living in the large rooms of his bungalow, during the day showing his clients ten and twelve-room houses, he dreams of living, sleeping, and eating in a single room, of having nothing but a bed, a dresser, a table, perhaps a small bookshelf in front of the window, where in summer the phlox can be seen . . .

Once his grandmother made him pancakes in the middle of the night. He had dreamed of pancakes and woke up, his grandmother woke too, and sang him a lullaby to help him go back to sleep, but he did not want to go back to sleep, he wanted pancakes. So, in her nightgown, braided hair down her back, she went into the kitchen. She brought him the pancakes on a wooden tray and sat down next to him and watched while he ate. He ate just half of the pancakes before falling right back to sleep.

When his grandmother was very old, she forgot her children and grandchildren and immersed herself in her own childhood. Her sons sat around her bed and learned the story of a nineteenth-century family of strangers.

But Mother, don't you know me? I'm your son, Heiner!

You're not my Heiner. My Heiner has beautiful black curls.

She was referring to her younger brother who had died of diphtheria seventy years ago.

At her funeral her coffin was open, the old women sitting on their chairs were thinking to themselves: so I have outlived you, by how much longer will I outlive you? and: What did you do with the years before this? What did I do? What does one do with one's life, the young Mommsen thought. Then the big door opened and the priest came in, dressed in white, accompanied by two acolytes, and behind him was a particularly sunny January day, with a particularly blue sky, and a particularly sunny blue breeze wafted through the chapel; so, for an early spring moment drunk with hope, he experienced an ethereal serenity; if such a thing can be, he thought, there can be no death; he sat up straight and faced the priest, who spoke of a death which cannot be and of an eternal life which follows from that, while the door to the sun had long since closed.

A Conversation at the Bar

He dreams that he is going into a hotel bar at the intersection of Hollywood and Vine. Mommsen recognizes it immediately although he has never been there before. He even knows the Gentleman sitting at the bar drinking a Tom Collins; a good-looking Gentleman of Mommsen's age. He gives the impression of being somewhat contemplative and distracted, but that does not fool Mommsen, he knows immediately Who he is dealing with.

At last! he calls out, may I join you? The Gentleman makes a friendly gesture toward the adjacent barstool. The same as the Gentleman's drinking, Mommsen says to the bartender, who is an older Froehlich, and then with reproach: No wonder You're so difficult to find, everyone's always looking for You somewhere up there . . . I know, the Gentleman says with his distracted smile, forever all-knowing, forever all-powerful. I as a human being, He says, would be reluctant to let a word like 'forever' pass My lips, when I can't even begin to imagine what it means. Don't you agree?

He conjures a green banknote onto the bar and slips down off His stool. One has one's phases, He says, isn't that right? Look around you: absolutely everything has its phases!

Mommsen wakes up; it is two in the morning and he is thirsty. He goes into the kitchen barefooted to get a mineral water from the refrigerator. On the outside sill, pressed up against the window pane, a big tiger-striped tomcat sits and watches, uninvolved. Leaning on the kitchen counter, water glass in hand, eye to eye with the strange tomcat, Mommsen recalls his first communion: a little boy in knee pants, his hands folded.

Well?

I swallowed God!

Aren't you happy?

I don't know. He'll always be there, knowing everything I do, and giving me orders.

You'll never be alone again. Isn't that wonderful?

Yes, it's wonderful. But what's going to happen when I want to be by myself?

Mommsen turns out the light. He feels lonely as he makes his way back to bed, downright deserted.

The Hippie

This afternoon for the first time in a long time Mommsen is standing in a church, but not as a tourist. The main altar may be a work of art, Mommsen is not concerned, for him the altar is what it was in his childhood, a shadowy place of sacrifice and clearly a throne of power.

He does not dare move very far forward, he realizes he needs an intercessor for this, his return. He steps up to one of the side altars where there are a dozen short red candles burning under the picture of a slender saint.

He makes an effort to pray. It is not easy, he does not even know the name of the saint, and it is difficult to ask a stranger for help: Whoever you are, whatever you may have done for the good of eternal life—I pray thee, who hast never heard of me, use even the tiniest part of thy power, thy faculty, for the benefit of my own lost soul . . .

Nothing happens. No consolation is forthcoming, no feeling. Mommsen tries to remember: he had it once, many years ago, he must be able to immerse himself in it again! It is probably a matter of patience. Mommsen sighs, the church is quiet, the sounds can be counted: once the groaning of a pew, then shuffling, a muted cough. His gaze is captured by the burning candles.

A whispered request gives him a start: Could you spare me a mark? The youth is still quite young, insofar as one can tell through the frizzy beard, a long-haired hippie in jeans and a loose-fitting shirt. To Mommsen he smells of beer, and what is more disgusting: he is smiling.

You've got beer on your breath!

No, the youth says.

Aren't you the least bit ashamed of begging for beer in a church? If I were you I'd get a job!

The youth backs away from Mommsen's disgusted whisper, he shakes his head in regret and is gone, without a sound, in tattered tennis shoes.

Mommsen is surprised at how angry this encounter has made him. What business is it of his whether the youth works or not, let him beg! He tries to relax, takes a deep breath of incense, looks at the flickering candles, looks up at the picture: Whoever you may be—the saint is standing there in sackcloth, slender, smiling, still very young, insofar as one can see through the frizzy beard—

It hits him like a brick: he feels dizzy, a sense of falling: the earth is opening up. He just stands there, paralyzed by shame. He should go and look for the youth, but he does not move from this spot. I pray thee, who hast never heard of me, use the smallest fragment of thy power, thy means. He wants to take his wallet out of his pocket and throw a mark into the alms box, a second, a third, everything he has with him, but he does not move, he just stands there under the smile of the young saint, for what seems a long time, until finally he gathers the strength to get up and leave.

The Bony Growth

In the morning he discovers a round lump on his right wrist, it can be moved around, back and forth like a marble; it does not hurt. Still he is aware of his disfigurement all day, in conversations he feels staring eyes drawn to the lump, he tries pulling his shirtcuff down over it, but the cuff keeps pulling up, revealing the growth which has become a visible sign of his inner disfigurement, a mark of shame.

He dreams of lumps spreading over his entire body, covering him with a bony cratered hide, like some prehistoric reptile. He expends much fruitless dream time counting up the lumps, he cannot finish the count. The following week he goes to the doctor.

Harmless, the doctor says, but if it bothers you I can remove it.

Who's going to guarantee that it won't come back again?

No one.

In that case, let's not bother.

He gets used to hiding his right hand; when he is alone he pushes the lump down into his wrist. When one of his molars begins to loosen, threatening to fall out, he sees this as a kind of compensation for his newly formed body part and for a time he is relieved. But the tooth roots itself again and the growth stays.

A Letter Arrives

" . . . have listed you as theme number one on our agenda and would like to ask you to answer the following questions: What significance does the celebration for Chaplain Schorr have for you—a change in the way you have lived your life until now? A breakthrough to something new? In what way? Do you believe that Chaplain Schorr wanted to become a martyr, and do you believe that a martyr can still be a role model for today's youth? How do you understand the motto Chaplain Schorr left behind: 'My eyes gaze upon the Lord. He will free my foot from the net'?"

He feels himself cornered. There is no way he can move unhindered. He feels he has been put on display, which means that everyone who looks at him, and these days everyone is looking at him, demands that he behave as if he were on display: role model, no flaws.

What others do once or twice a year, on their birthdays or at New Year's, and then only for about ten minutes, a glass of champagne in hand, he must do every day: look around, get his bearings, ask himself: Where am I? How far have I come? What have I done to give my life meaning? What am I doing, what will I do?—And no chance to set the glass down and get on with the agenda, because whatever may be on his agenda, it will not be enough.

And the fear that he has left something out, forgotten something he was supposed to do, without actually knowing what it was, that is the worst, the fog: there is nothing for him to hold on to.

Then he thinks: there must certainly be something totally

appropriate for someone in precisely this situation, something he should do to fulfill the hope vested in him, why else would all this have come about, and then he looks around and finds nothing: maybe it is a lack of imagination, he simply cannot imagine what he should do in precisely this situation: should he change his life? How? And he dreads the day when it will happen for the second time, when it is finally over and he will have to say: Too bad. Whatever intent or design there may have been for my life: I did not fulfill it; I failed.

Hobby

He would like to have had a hobby; he envies people who bring out their stamp collections or their coin collections in the evening, or go out with their bowling team, their riding club, their hunting club. He tried unsuccessfully to develop an interest in golf, succulents, amphora. Even the narrowest of fields would have sufficed if he could have mastered it. It would have provided him with an external perspective from which he could view the chaos, and he would have been able to tell himself: just as here in my little domain, somehow everything out there will make sense. It would have made the world, at least in this tiny sector, comprehensible.

Piranhas

They sleep separately now. Morning sleep escapes him, as they say. By four his night is over, he sits straight up in bed, soaked in sweat, his pulse racing. Again and again catastrophe propels him out of his sleep: the last steps in the last courtyard, the firing squad. He knows the abyss is waiting for him and that there is no way to escape; no question, he will have to descend into it. He gets up, opens the drapes and then falls back into his own gray dawn, in this room, seemingly hung with spider webs, which he thinks of as the realm of the semi-somnolent.

The chaplain on death row: a king among beggars. For him death was no catastrophe, isn't that right?

And the others: if they had known that he was going to die for you—what would they have done? Wouldn't they have screamed: Take me! Take me?

He is walking across a frozen lake, and the ice is getting thinner and thinner; finally it is as if he were walking on water, that gives him an enormous sense of self-confidence for one, two, three steps before he begins to sink.

Below are the piranhas; he is swimming in the middle of a school, and when one of them comes so close to his face that he can hear it, he cries out: they're going to eat me! They're going to eat me up!—That'd be awful, the fish says, but you don't have to be afraid of me, I'm not like that, I only want a tiny bite. That said, the piranha bites off his nose, and as the others swim by they each take a tiny bite, and—swoosh—he is a skeleton shedding salty tears into the sea, he knows it will take years to get all that muscle back.

The long road to morning: passing along so close to damnation.

Two Men at the Door

They are standing in the doorway to the breakfast room, they look around, they are looking for Mommsen. In hats and coats, that is what makes them so frightening, and that there are two of them. The beadles. Such an old-fashioned word. There have always been such men, emissaries of an anonymous power. So conspicuously inconspicuous. Force flows unhindered through the emptiness of their faces, pushing him against the back of his chair. The room is full of people, they are sitting at small tables drinking grapefruit juice, they throw their heads back exposing their throats, no thoughts of strangulation or knives, they have become jaded to any sort of danger, ready for the end. Above all: they are no protection. They are the same people who sit quietly on the train and watch while one of them is dragged to his feet and then beaten down to the floor. And if they are dragged from their seats themselves and beaten, they are not surprised when no one comes to their rescue, they simply accept violence: amazed, not that such violence occurs, only that this time they have been targeted.

Until a jackboot to the temple delivers forgetfulness, beloved darkness.

He does not dare wipe his brow here at the table, under Nina's watchful eye, so he takes his napkin and casually touches it to the moist area between his mouth and his nose, the two gentlemen approach smiling, they even bow, and as he stands up distracted by the weakness in his knees, they introduce themselves: a member of the city council and a church deacon, they are here to pick him up for the ceremony, they would like to extend a most cordial welcome.

A Semisomnolent State

This is a transition between two sleep states which, apart from his person, have only one thing in common: their equally great distance from reality. A no-man's-land with the danger and the unrest and the hope of boundary regions.

He is at home in this time of the day as if time had become place.

The postman, wearing a field-gray uniform, arrives and gives him a package wrapped in blue ribbons like a present. With outstretched arms Mommsen holds it away from himself and protests: I simply cannot accept this!

You have to, the postman says, it's addressed to you.

But I have no idea why it was sent to me, you'll have to take it back.

I can't.

Mommsen listens: It's ticking!

Everything ticks, the postman says as he leaves.

Morning draws across the sky, a pink contrail in the form of a flattened parabola, a trajectory into a vacuum. Mommsen, walled in by his black fears, notices only when they drop away that he was not walled in at all, but was blind. Or not even that: he had simply opened his eyes too soon, it was still night. Amazed, he observes how a tangled coil in his brain is unwinding, releasing a dazzling phosphorescent light which slowly and emphatically closes down again. After that he sees his brain through new eyes: as a tightly-curled bud with hundreds of layers, full of indescribable latent light energy, a dormant beam, which once exposed would light up the world.

For him the house is running down like a clock. He notices it getting slower and knows: it will be over soon. And a joyous mood of change takes hold of him, anticipation, release.

The clock ticks on and on, he hardly hears it any more, but then it suddenly stops and he hears it has stopped and knows: the clock has run down, that frightens him and pleases him, just as it frightens him and pleases him that a place where he has lived for decades is absolutely alien.

Finally the sun rises unusually fast, it seems to him, in leaps and bounds. As if on an eastward flight: every time he looks at the sun it is another step higher. And again the quiet amazement that it has after all become day once more.

Mommsen gets up. His alarm clock is ticking. It is orange and shaped like a diving bell, he bought it on a sunny day in Berlin on the shores of the Lietzensee.

Wake Up!

The terrible unease, the weariness: Mommsen goes about beginning a day. He knows the ritual, he knows how one begins days. In the kitchen he stands in front of the coffeepot, coffee measure in hand, his gaze turned to the colorless garden, then back to the filter holder made of heatproof glass. He puts the measure back into the coffee canister, closes the lid, puts the canister back into the cupboard and closes the cupboard door.

A voice calls out: Wake up!

He opens the door to Nina's room: Are you still sleeping? I'm leaving now!—closes the door to Nina's room, opens the house door, closes it, opens the garage door, opens the car door, closes it, drives the car out into the street, opens the car door, closes it, closes the garage door, opens the car door, closes it and drives, just as he does every day, to his office, first along a street lined with gardens, then along another street where gardens are planned, and then along a third street which used to be lined with gardens but is now the site of an unfinished development. After that he gets into city traffic, stop-and-go then crawling again, finally into the underground garage in the basement of his office building. Mommsen turns the key, listens for the sound of the motor, the motor goes silent.

A voice calls out: Wake up!

Most of all he fears: that he will close his eyes and open them again, and see when he opens them that since he closed his eyes, not hours but years have passed, his entire life.

A Game by Day

Mommsen is not interested in going to work any more. A kind of boredom has overtaken him, it gets worse every day and finally turns into fear. He is afraid of people, especially his customers. To him their thoughts seem unbearably tedious, they have a suffocating emptiness.

A fear of death comes over him: these people are stealing his existence, piece by irrevocable piece, against his will and without a trace of real gain to him, they are bringing him one step closer to death.

In a certain sense, Mommsen says, they are my murderers.

His clients, of all people!

And he thought Nina was crazy.

He spends his working hours playing games. He forbids any interruption, closes the door and pulls a chair up to the table where he keeps the model townhouses. He sets up trees, shrubs, swings and fountains. He places little animals, cats, dogs, and parrots among the greenery and here and there a small wooden carving of a human; he's careful with these figures, he only has three, a man reading a book, a second man sunbathing, and a woman in a white dress who is simply standing there. These people have no connection to one another, the men are busy reading and sunbathing, the woman is carrying an empty basket on her arm and seems to be thinking: What now? Mommsen puts her at an observation point on the uppermost terrace, he sets out two yew trees and a pine and puts a white cat down in the grass at her feet.

Don't Forget Maruschka

What fascinates me about your situation is the fact that there's no way out of it. I've been thinking: I don't see any real options for you.

They are sitting in a beer garden under chestnut trees hung with lanterns.

I know that should frighten me, Mommsen says.

The moment you accepted the sacrifice, or became aware of it, every door around you closed. First: You can't continue to live the way you've been living, the sacrifice demands more. Second: You can't lead a saintly life, you'll have to excuse me, but you have inadequate resources. Third: You can't sacrifice yourself for another person, you wouldn't be settling your debt, you'd merely be passing it along. Fourth: You can't take your own life because then the priest's good deed would be reduced ad absurdum. Fifth—

Please, stop.

Right. You've resigned yourself. Naturally, that would be an option but it's the one you can afford least of all.

I am not my brother's keeper, I am the one who was saved. No one thinks about him, how he feels. Must he be grateful to his brother? Or can he simply accept it as a matter of course that he has been saved? Maybe he doesn't even want to be saved, maybe he'd just prefer to die!

The waitress brings two unordered glasses of beer.

I'm sorry but I don't have any feelings, I can't even remember any. At most I might be able to invent some for your benefit.

But you long for a feeling.

No, Mommsen says. I'm not even capable of imagining a desire, let alone feeling one.

The men in the beer garden have rolled up their sleeves and are sitting around a table singing: *She was the prettiest maid of all, in all of Poland, but no, but no, she spoke, never a kiss from me . . .*

No one is forcing you to feel anything, Froehlich says, you should simply remember what happened thirty-five years ago, that's all.

As if blown away.

And the years after that, the five-times-seven years? Odd, that you don't remember! It's as if you just didn't want to remember!

Mommsen does not know what to say, he shrugs his shoulders; at some time over the course of these years he must have died, unbeknownst to himself and everyone else. He is a little embarrassed, nothing more.

The men at the large table are singing: Don't forget Maruschka—*Vergiß Maruschka nicht, das Polenkind . . .*

You know this old song from the war?

Of course, Mommsen says, I know it well. He is surprised at the raw tone in his voice, it sounds as if there were a second being whom he normally does not allow to speak.

You're touched, Froehlich says.

Nothing Helps and Nothing Hurts

He walks through the city in the direction of his office and passes it by. The thousands of times he has walked toward his office and not once, until today, has he passed it by.

At this stage he feels as well as he usually does, as far as he can remember, that is, because just this is an indication of his condition: that he hardly remembers anything. This mild amnesia, which he refers to as his weak memory, is simply the prerequisite for his well-being.

Mommsen loves this quiet as he loves fields of snow and cool autumn mornings when mists swallow up his feet, and he feels himself float.

Amazing how easy it is to live with such a tiny fraction of awareness, somehow weightless.

The euphoria of the urban morning consists in equal parts of inner emptiness, physical well-being, stage setting. The setting consists of towers, gables and painted facades, flowers growing out of concrete vases; model houses, scenery.

Mommsen yawns. His sense perceptions begin to bore him. What should he make of this make-believe? The perpetually wasted energy, spent only to remain aware of this suspect panorama, the imperative to constantly perceive . . . One day it will explode along with a small artery in his brain . . . Suffering millions of explosions, the earth keeps turning, still young and fragile . . .

Cotton batting in his head. Nothing helps and nothing hurts.

"After thirty-five years the eighty-year-old Venetian, Luigi Sardi, killed the policeman who had arrested him in 1947. Sardi, a gondolier at the time, had robbed a woman, murdered her, cut up her body, put it in a suitcase and thrown it into the lagoon."

An experiment: raise your eyes, look at the rooftops, the sky. No one else does that. Everyone else looks down at the asphalt in front of them, sideways at store windows, into the eyes of oncoming pedestrians, at the backs of those walking in front of them. No one looks up, no one sees what Mommsen sees there, his sweet secret emptiness.

"This is a case that should be of interest not only to the church, but also to youth, to the entire public. Finally, despite the negative, destructive, disheartening and threatening aspects of our lives today, this is a case which gives cause for hope."

In the Maw of the Crocodile

One day he went down a street like this one, under an all-too-blue sky, and the end of the street rose up to meet him like a threat signifying the end of the afternoon, and suddenly he stopped and turned around believing that his footprints must be burned into the asphalt, but he could see nothing and the end of the street was the end of that afternoon, and afterwards there was nothing more, no feeling, nothing.

Still he is a little frightened: a man who has just walked through a meadow full of flowers turns around only to discover a gaping crater there where he has just passed.

He believes that he has lost something essential, that not being able to react he is not really alive.

"People today, confronted with their opportunities—for the most part lost. People who dare to begin anew . . . "

But Mommsen has no desire to take even the slightest risk. He finds himself in the maw of the crocodile. He has settled in, he knows every tooth. He knows that only the sides are dangerous and that nothing can happen to him as long as he stays in the middle.

"Our Milky Way galaxy is racing through space at the unexpectedly high speed of 1.6 million kilometers per hour. This is according to calculations done by astronomers at the University of California on measurements of cosmic background radiation, which, according to currently accepted theory, resulted from the Big Bang, the event which initiated the expansion of the universe fifteen billion years ago."

How do you feel having just survived a leap from the Eiffel Tower, having become the third richest man in Cincinnati overnight, having just won the Super Lotto and lost your ticket? How do you feel?

He walks and walks; like someone who is trying to get tired, hoping then to be able to fall asleep. But it is still daytime. The sun is shining.

Simply unbelievable how little he takes in, nothing actually.

Suddenly the fear that before he gets to the subway station his purpose will abandon him, or more to the point, his will to catch the train, to go home or anywhere else at all.

At the entrance to the station he stops and leans against a pillar and watches an everchanging stream of faces being carried up the escalator. Their faces are bright as they emerge into the sunlight, but he suddenly begins to see individuals among them with black marks on their foreheads, the print of a giant thumb which apparently has descended from the clouds: there a man, there a child, here a woman again . . . They step easily from the escalator onto firm ground and push on, marked as they are, and unaware.

Fate? Nina asks this evening, how so: In the sense of bowed legs, a drunken father, an undesirable skin color, a long and happy marriage? Don't talk to me about fate, she says. If there were such a thing, then everything would be different.

Do you think so?

I know it.

On the Bridge

Something has changed: What? Objects are still there, so are people, he has only to reach out his hand. But when he does they retreat. Mommsen has lost himself, he has lived himself into disintegration.

Once things have reached this point, Mommsen is surprised to find the feeling somewhere between painless and pleasant. All of a sudden it is so much easier to leave than to stay.

He recognizes this from the fact that he is no longer afraid: In the morning in the underground garage of his office building Mommsen leaves his car and walks through the gray light between the pillars and bays to the exit which leads to the stairway. He has the habit of holding his breath and walking faster as he approaches the second pillar, every time at this place he is attacked by an image: a man behind a ledge, his arm raised, holding a tire wrench. The ideal setup for a murder, the murderer has time to take valuables from his victim, get into his car and drive away up the unguarded exit ramp.

This morning Mommsen neither holds his breath nor walks faster. Of course he does think about the man with the wrench, but briefly, and he does not care whether the murderer is standing there or not. He is filled with a new serenity, the reward for having lost his fear of death. With a spring in his step he leaves the new-age catacomb, and only when he gets to his desk and sees the bundles of files is he overcome again with a heaviness, an awful sadness, a sense of things passing.

In the evening he is standing on a bridge where many others have also stood, actually it is much more a terminal than a bridge: will he jump? He thinks through every possible objection: what can be said against it? He is surprised that suicidal people ever allow themselves to be talked out of it: there is no convincing argument against suicide. A responsibility to the living? Seen from such a tall bridge the details get lost. He will not be able to support Nina any longer, well then: she will support herself. She will get a job and be all the healthier for it. And if the shock should throw her off balance she will just have to catch herself, and if not, well then she will have the same unburdened exit available to her as he now has at this moment. No, he has no responsibility to the living.

Mommsen notices that he can no longer feel his hands. They are lying on the railing like two alien objects, they differ neither in color nor in temperature from the rusty iron. For a moment he is convinced that they are a part of the railing and not a part of him.

Mommsen picks his hands up from the railing and rubs them warm, he shifts his weight from one foot to the other and walks slowly toward the stairs. There is a policeman standing at the end of the bridge, he looks Mommsen over carefully, greets him, calling out: an unpleasant place, isn't it? You're very right, Mommsen says, and notices in passing that, next to the radio the policeman is carrying at his chest, he also has a pair of binoculars. Night vision binoculars, he is certain.

Flirting with Death

It is the great allure of death that fills him body and soul. For many years, it now seems to him, there has been no temptation as sweet and as strong as this one. He will not ever again talk about the poor desperate ones who are driven to their deaths. We are not driven to our death, we are lured into it.

Mommsen, sitting in his car on the way to his office, is driving along the road next to a suburban train; the two routes cross shortly before entering the city. He recognizes the tired, indifferent faces of commuters behind the windows of the train. He would like to honk loudly and yell out to them: Good news, people! You don't have to put up with this if you don't want to! You can end it all this very minute: door open, jump out, nothing easier than that, child's play! Actually they should know it themselves. The signal light at the railroad crossing is red, he lets his foot choose between the accelerator and the brakes. His foot chooses the brakes, Mommsen is unconcerned. When the escape route is open, right, there is no need to hurry.

The Sin

Instead he gets drunk. He begins the evening in a tavern he found while looking for someone to rescue, he ends up much after midnight in a bar that reminds him dimly of the hotel bar in his dream. He climbs up onto a barstool and looks around: the place is packed, but the Gentleman from his dream is not among the guests.

Mommsen orders a Tom Collins and then another; maybe a third one. He knows nothing after that.

He wakes up on a mattress in a room where three young women are sitting on the floor playing cards, while a fourth is listening to music through extremely large headphones. They all have long hair and are wearing loose-fitting garments.

One of the girls who seems vaguely familiar to him says, without interrupting her game: Well, this guy told me a story from the last war, a really good one. How they wanted to blow up a bridge and were caught, and how afterwards when they were sitting in a cell knowing that it was all over and talking about how it really was worth it, at least they risked their lives for a good cause, the others hadn't even done that, and this guy says he wanted to feel that way, but he hadn't really wanted to take part, he was afraid, it was only by accident that he'd been there, and how there was a priest in the cell too, who had preached against the war and was listening to them talk, and how he tells the guard that he wants to be taken to the commandant, and how, when they're picked up the next morning, the priest goes and lets himself be shot in this guy's place.

Great stuff, says the girl with the headphones hanging around her neck; and now he's out getting tanked.

He got it from the newspaper, one of the others says, there was a story a while ago, I read it myself.

What a winner, says Mommsen's acquaintance. And then he says he can't come to terms with all this and that he's always tried to be good but he just can't get it together, and that now he wants to commit a real sin, so he finally does something, anything. Crazy, huh?

The girl with the headphones asks: Sin? What does he mean?

I don't know, he didn't say. He probably doesn't know himself.

Amazed, the girl with the headphones stares at him.

As if he were some rare animal, Mommsen thinks to himself on the way home after this adventure; he wants to laugh but he cannot.

How has it come to this, Nina says, after twenty-two years the gentleman has started spending nights away from home: and not a trace of remorse?

It is almost noon, they are standing across from one another in the kitchen between the stove and the dishwasher. The situation is as old as the institution, the threats of millennia are hanging in the air, dungeon, pillory, stoning. That these punishments have been administered only to women does not seem a help to Mommsen: proof that he is a man of the twentieth century, however obviously a man of the first half.

Remorse just doesn't work anymore, Mommsen says. But I can still remember the daily pangs of guilt at bedtime: you didn't go to church and our Dear Lord was very sad . . . You stole a gummi bear and God cried. You hit your mother and God turned His Visage away from you.—And somehow this old man, who's forever feeling himself insulted, is supposed to have enough intelligence and humor to create even a centipede?

My, my, Nina says, this is interesting.

She looks him in the eye for the first time in months, it seems to Mommsen, and for the first time she is not being watchful, but attentive, almost cheerful: what's happening here? Is something finally happening?

Mommsen goes to the bathroom to get an Alka Seltzer.

The Protest

Mommsen says: I'm not playing along with this anymore! The endless mean questions: What's he thinking, how's he behaving? What has he ever been? What have his deeds been worth: not much? Or something? And how much! Having to justify myself at every turn; why should I? Since last April I've done nothing but run a gauntlet of wagging fingers!

They are sitting in an outdoor café in midsummer heat under a blue and yellow striped umbrella.

As far as I'm concerned, you can relax, this is the last time. Next week my report's going to press and you'll be rid of me.

I know how you're going to portray me: as a failure who got lucky. But if I really failed, then so did the priest: he made a mistake, he died for the wrong man. And the memories you're always looking for: can you tell me exactly how you've spent the last thirty-five years?

I'm only twenty-eight, says Froehlich, and I really do know—

But not for much longer. Another hour with Mommsen at a table in this café and he will not know what he has done with his twenty-eight years, and more importantly, to what end.

Deeds! Mommsen says. I haven't even been able to tell good ones from bad, let alone commit a real sin.

I don't know what you're talking about. The only sins committed these days are the ones we all commit together.

They look into the street. Streams of gleaming cars pour into the city, out of the city, shimmering exhaust gases among the poplars.

That's too anonymous for me, it doesn't really hit home. It's carelessness, an outrage, stupidity, but not a sin.

The Monstrous Animal

And what about your conscience?

Conscience! The genuinely bad things I've done in my life, I've done to soothe my conscience. My own father, I didn't let him die.—One more drop? the doctor asked, by this time even he was skeptical, this will get him through the next week; after that there's very little hope. I saw his eyes rolled up in his head, white in his white face, I thought: he's pleading, but what's he pleading for? I asked: Father! You want to live? Doesn't everyone want to live? I don't know if he heard me.

I felt my conscience. That monstrous animal: it is going to swoop down on me if I let my father die, it will lay my father's death at my feet. Old curses recalled: the devil take you! I can't afford to let him die, I've got to keep him going.—One more week, I said, we'll give him one more precious week.

Very good, said my conscience, he who loves his father extends his father's life. I know now that my father wanted to die, he was pleading for death to come, but I didn't want to hear him; I had to soothe my conscience.

In other words, says Froehlich, you gave up looking for meaning, you rescued yourself, like the old story about the bank messenger, you know: a messenger is sent from one bank to another with a locked case without knowing what's in the case. He only knows that he's covered a certain distance—the reason, the goal and the consequences of his assignment are unknown to him. The case may even be empty but he's sent out because he's a messenger, there's a certain mechanism at work. Maybe he's carrying a fortune.

In any case: what does he do? He says to himself: since I don't know why I'm on this assignment, at least I'll make the best of this hour! So he begins by taking care of a little personal business, treats himself to a beer, takes a stroll in the sun— does things he normally wouldn't enjoy half so much.—Now, you see, this hour is yours!

Perhaps, says Mommsen, but one hour is not much in a whole, long day.

Other People Die Too

I'm tired of being the guilty one because I haven't made anything of a life that was given me. Given not once but twice. I didn't ask for it either time.

Let's agree on one thing: Simply being born places no requirements on us. There is no power to whom we owe a fulfilled life. If anything, an unsolicited gift requires a polite expression of thanks, that's all. That's what you mean, isn't it?

Why are you asking me? Ask yourself for once! You're a Christian, aren't you? Someone died for you too, isn't that right? And what are you doing about it? Admit it, you haven't done a thing. You'll say: He didn't single me out, He died for all of us. You'll hide in the crowd. As if a crowd ever was a place to hide!

Maybe the priest didn't single me out either. Maybe he wasn't really concerned with saving another life but with fulfilling his own? And at my expense he's become a martyr, the most noble of egotists?

They are sitting in exhaust gases. The stream of cars continues to pour into the city and out of the city; from time to time a red traffic light brings them to a halt.

There's no way getting around it, you owe him your life.

Mommsen says: I don't want to hear about it anymore. Life, sacrifice it, maintain it, give it, give it away, extend it, cast it away. . . Life from where; life to what end? Life for what, for whom, and why!

Shall I tell you the truth? I don't give a damn! How, why, even if, I'm alive, or whether you think this in any way extraordinary, crazy or even criminal.

By all rights at the age of twenty I was a dead man; I've been a dead man ever since. Well? Other people die too. Why should I have to be so full of thanks? What I really got out of this was: an awful debt, a tortured conscience, the obligation to find meaning where there is none, a later death instead of an early one, with all that entails: old age, illness and decay, hellish boredom. I'd have to be some kind of genius to rise above all this, and even then . . .

Of course the priest was a great man, a martyr, a hero, but: he became all that through me; only because he sacrificed himself for me. He needed me for his act of heroism in the same way I needed him for my continued existence.

And what about your oft professed gratitude? "I will be forever thankful"—I've got that down in fourteen different places.

My gratitude has shifted, that's all. I'm still thankful, but not just to the priest.

This is the first time you haven't been depressed by a talk with Froehlich, Nina says. What did he ask you?

Not much.

Well, how about you, what did you tell him?

Different things, all kinds of things.

Aha, she says. Then out of the blue: We haven't even thought about a vacation. I'd really like to go someplace new with you, up north or somewhere west—Mommsen hesitates.

You're not interested, Nina says, all you want to do is go back to the same old south.

Once and for All

A trip with Nina to the seashore is all trips with Nina to the seashore, for Mommsen the many times have melded into one time, including the present. Maybe he is only going there again so he won't have to store away any new memories? A trip to the seashore is as good as no trip at all; everything is the way it was, once and forever.

This time and always there is the highway bridge in the mountains on the way south, so high it makes him dizzy and still only half finished, Mommsen sees it from the old road, haunting alpine reverie, the danger of a sudden plunge into the gorge. In the meantime of course the bridge has been completed, they cross it every year, twice, four times and more, but for Mommsen it is still the tenuous scaffolding of the past, a ramp into the sky. Every time he passes the midpoint, he risks plunging into the abyss, and each time wonder of wonders he reaches the other side.

Once, Nina is sitting on the promenade in Lazise, her

hands folded in her lap, with the lost expression of a woman on vacation with the wrong man.

Music breaks out of the mists on the lake, the rhythms of a percussive piano; it seems a vaguely familiar melody to Mommsen as if he might have heard it in a dream, then the outline of a ship emerges. It is an old paddle-wheel with three decks stacked up one over the other; the piano player is on the top deck under a canopy, behind him a couple dancing in short, staccato steps. Through the windows on the middle deck two waiters dressed in white can be seen looking after guests.

The steamer glides silently up to the landing, a crewman jumps onto the dock and runs a line around the mooring, from the bridge three officers in blue observe the few passengers who are coming on board. Everything proceeds with a mute solemnity, the piano player hammers out his monotone melody, the guests quietly spread out over the lower deck, a woman lifts her small child into her lap and holds him tightly as if she believed him to be in danger, the crewman unties the line and jumps on board, two officers disappear from the window of the conning tower, the waiters still press their faces to the windows, on the top deck the couple dances on tirelessly, silently as it came the steamer glides away from the shore back out onto the lake, on the deck a woman in a blue dress takes off her straw hat, raises and lowers it at the end of an outstretched arm in the direction of a now completely abandoned landing, accompanied by its mechanical music the ship disappears into the mists.

To Mommsen it is as if the steamer had landed for his benefit alone and was now moving along on its uncompleted mission. He should not have let that happen.

We missed it, Nina says.

The Island

Once, there was also an island in the blue water, from a distance only a green hill, but later a breakwater made of fieldstone surrounding a small harbor and beyond a few houses, scattered trees up along the cliff, on top a gray church. A woman cooking soup; at the stroke of twelve noon she took the pot off the stove and went to the window.

Women, children, old men and young boys were all standing on the breakwater. The children played among the rocks, two tiny puppies scampered along with them, the grownups stood in groups and talked. They were all wearing hats to protect themselves from the midday sun. No one showed any sign of impatience.

Then, as in a fairy tale, the yacht emerged out of the mists along the horizon, white flanks out of the spray, the people on the breakwater shaded their eyes from the sun and watched how it grew, a young man ran to the second house on the harbor and came back with the old woman on his arm, she was wearing a white headscarf and an apron and walked proudly, stooped over, stopped among the others, they moved back a step so that like a queen she was encircled by reverent subjects, she was the mother of this wonder that sailed every year over the big pond into their tiny harbor, for a few weeks lifted the village out of the poverty of its island existence into prosperity, paradise with American names, slapped fresh paint onto the houses, laid sod around the boccie court, set out benches, restored what was in decay, provided new nets, and clothed little girls in bright frocks and little boys in fashionable athletic wear: a heavenly project for Mr. Vukcic from Boston with his too-thin wife, who spent her days on a styrofoam mat at the beach, and his three wild children, who conquered the island with loud screams, fought with cats and dogs, while Mr. Vukcic, Stepan, went from family to family and cleverly distributed his money, modernized without ruining, involved himself with cares that never seemed too trivial, recorded notes in his notebook, bowled on the meadow, and for the rest of the time was satisfied to sit in a low room across the table from his taciturn mother and wait for a smile from her stern face, or to accompany her on her daily rounds to the cemetery, where they stood silently at the grave of his brother, who at the age of nineteen was struck by lightning, a handsome happy youth for whom the old woman would even today exchange Stepan, the older son, along with his yacht and money and everything he had done and would still do for the island. No, he had never been her favorite.

Another time, the barren cliffs along the shore, the tiny islands; the sea, polished smooth as a stone, is holding its breath, not a sound, no movement, not even the smallest wave striking the hull. Only a pulse in the veins, a humming in the head, fear.

The stillness of the dead is loud by comparison.

Finally a fish flies, the spell is broken. They start up the motor and leave, foam on the bow and the wake out behind slowly opening into a fan. Three miles farther on and the calms are forgotten, the water rippling in the sun, a sport boat roars alongside, the man holds up his catch, the baby shark. Two hundred meters of line and a mackerel for bait, that's the whole secret. White stomach, pinkish fins, squared-off jaw, streamline form of utmost simplicity, deadly elegance.

Strange that all Mommsen's memories seem to be associated with water, flowing water, frozen water, as if there were no other elements, air for example, or earth. And ships that emerge from the fog, bridges, and old ladies—

The Event

It is still light when they arrive. Mommsen parks the car on the promenade and walks the few steps down to the water. For a minute he observes the repeatedly frustrated attempt of the waves to take a definite form, until finally the sight of so much patience becomes too much for him, and he goes back to the street.

They drive to their old hotel, take their old room on the second floor with a view of two palms, laurel branches and, from between two walls, a sliver of the sea.

The weather is fair; they get up late, take a leisurely breakfast, and spend most of the hours of the day on the beach. There on the afternoon of the first of October the momentous event: one blow, and the whole stage set comes tumbling down.

Mommsen opens his eyes. Sun above, sand below, in front of him water, water, water, everything as if painted on black— this whole extraordinary artifice he had settled into with such innocence suddenly admits its animosity and spits in his face. Mommsen has one intense wish: to spit back. No one notices.

He looks up and down the beachfront: a mass of props, beach umbrellas, lounge chairs, among them humans in striking poses leaping after balls, pawing in the sand. It does not seem to bother them that under a thin top layer the sand is damp and dark, thus exposing the entire sundrenched countryside all around as an illusion, as a dissembling, smiling skin stretched over an endless morass.

In front of him in the sand Mommsen sees a row of red toenails, a smooth leg, a piece of cloth, yellow daisies on a white background, and half of a tanned arm in front of a newspaper. He wonders what use all this might be.

I knew it, Nina says, they're stagnating but they haven't started to fall.

This observation takes his breath away, not because of the content, he knows immediately that it is a report on real estate prices, but because of the fact that Nina can speak, and that she is indeed Nina. Lying there on her blanket as she is, she could just as well be a stray animal, or a shiny brown ornament.

She stretches; her arms are whiter on the inside than they

are on the outside, at the edge of her bathing suit there is a thin white strip. It suddenly occurs to Mommsen that this two-toned bundle of skin and muscle is attached to its name as if to a fishhook, he can grasp onto it and take it with him.

Nina, let's go.

And she does come along.

Walking across the seawall on the way back to the hotel, he takes off his sunglasses and looks at the field of straw hats worn by tourists, swaying over the promenade, the ancient shutters on the houses, and above, the blue mists beyond which lies endless night; the overpowering absence of everything. He is filled with a tremendous serenity, a surprised laughter that he can hold back only with great effort. It is as if after a lifelong joke, he finally has got the point.

It's Really Very Simple

In the Hollywood swing in the front garden of their hotel where they drink espresso every afternoon, in the rhythm of the gentle back and forth, sing-song words reach his ear: yesterday—tomorrow—the day after tomorrow. The nonsense of the passing of time is suddenly obvious; it seems to him that the illusion he has suffered under is made up of a kaleidoscope of short-term hopes: hope for the next day, hope for passing an exam, hope for a good job, hope for a marriage, a house, a vacation at the seashore . . . All of a sudden, in the middle of it all, it is over; he has stopped hoping.

Maybe, Nina says, we should sell the bungalow and look for one of those old houses.

Fine, but there's no hurry.

I want you to feel yourself at home.

Mommsen accepts this gratefully, but he smiles and looks as if he has just heard a foreign word he doesn't understand.

That's right, he says, at home.

In the evening they drive along the coast. They stop at an outlook. There is light everywhere, but only in points. The context is clear: the lights surrounding them and over them, fireflies and stars, are wandering toward the horizon where they are swallowed up by the sea and carried into coves along the coast, where they become the lights below.

It's a very simple system, Mommsen says.

You're so cheerful! Nina says.

Mommsen is filled with an immense laugh.